Barbie and The Three Musketeers

By Mary Man-Kong
Based on the original screenplay by Amy Wolfram
Illustrated by Ulkutay Design Group and Allan Choi

Special thanks to Vicki Jaeger, Monica Okazaki, Tanya Mann, Christine Chang,
Rob Hudnut, Shelley Dvi-Vardhana, Jennifer Twiner McCarron, Pat Link,
Shawn McCorkindale, Walter P. Martishius, Tulin Ulkutay, and Ayse Ulkutay

A GOLDEN BOOK · NEW YORK

Educators and librarians, for a variety of teaching tools, visit us at www.randomhouse.com/teachers
Library of Congress Control Number: 2009925078   ISBN: 978-0-375-85448-4
Printed in the United States of America   10 9 8 7 6 5 4 3 2 1

Long ago, in a small village in France, there lived
a beautiful girl named Corinne. Every day, Corinne
practiced her fencing with her pet kitten, Miette.

"*En garde!*" Corinne cried as she swung her broom
like a sword. She dreamed of one day becoming a
Musketeer—a special protector of the royal family.

Corinne soon set off for Paris with Miette. But once she arrived, Corinne was told that girls could not be Musketeers. She was heartbroken!

Just then, a dog started chasing Miette. Corinne ran after them. She was in such a rush that she ran right into a puddle and splashed past a girl named Viveca.

Then Corinne bumped into a girl named Aramina . . .

and knocked over another girl named Renée.

Corinne finally caught Miette near the castle, where she was offered a job as a maid. With nowhere else to go, Corinne accepted.

The other maids were not very happy to meet Corinne—they were the three girls she had splashed, bumped, and knocked over! Luckily, they forgave Corinne, and they all became friends.

Meanwhile, preparations for a masquerade ball were under way. The ball was to be a celebration in honor of Prince Louis, who was going to be crowned king. But the prince's royal advisor, Philippe, had other ideas. Philippe wanted to be king himself, and he was secretly plotting to overthrow the prince.

One day, as Prince Louis walked through the castle's great hall, the ceiling started to collapse! The four girls sprang into action. Corinne used her duster as a sword to smash the falling stones. Viveca used her towel to crack bricks. Aramina kicked rocks. And Renée used her duster to shatter broken glass. Everyone was saved!

Corinne, Viveca, Renée, and Aramina were amazed by each other's skills. And the girls soon discovered that they shared the dream of becoming a Musketeer!

Hélène, an old housekeeper, overheard the girls and told them to follow her. She led them down a long, dark hall to a secret door. Behind it was the Musketeers' old training room!

"Do you think you can be Musketeers?" Hélène asked.

The girls couldn't wait to start their training!

Corinne, Viveca, Aramina, and Renée practiced every day.

"People still believe that girls cannot be Musketeers," said Hélène. "It's up to you to prove them wrong."

One afternoon, the girls heard someone cry for help.

A rope on Prince Louis's hot-air balloon had mysteriously been cut—and he was dangling from it dangerously!

Wasting no time, Corinne swung out the castle window and helped the prince back into his balloon.

"Thank you," Prince Louis said. He had never met a girl as brave and daring as Corinne. And Corinne had never met anyone as kind and brilliant as the prince. As they floated over Paris together, they began to fall in love.

Later that day, Corinne noticed men unloading boxes for the masquerade ball. Inside were real swords!

Corinne tried to warn Philippe and the castle guards that the prince was in danger. But Philippe didn't listen—and he banished Corinne and her friends from the castle forever.

The girls would not let that stop them from protecting Prince Louis!

"All for one and one for all!" they cried, joining hands.

Viveca designed four costumes. Then Aramina taught everyone how to dance, and Renée sketched a map of the castle.

"We can do this!" said Corinne.

Corinne, Viveca, Renée, and Aramina disguised themselves in glittering gowns. The guards didn't recognize them as they entered the castle for the masquerade ball.

Prince Louis was amazed by Corinne's beauty and chose her for the first dance. "You look familiar," said the prince. "Do I know you?"

Suddenly, Philippe and his men surrounded the prince with their swords!

But the four friends were ready!
"Prepare for battle!" Corrine shouted.
The girls used their swords, ribbons, fans, and
bow and arrow to stop Philippe's men.

During the commotion, Philippe kidnapped the prince and took him to the castle's rooftop. Luckily, Corinne spotted them and followed.

"You will never be king!" Corinne told Philippe.

Philippe raised his sword, but Corinne quickly defeated him with her fencing skills.

To reward their bravery, King Louis declared that Corinne, Viveca, Renée, and Aramina were Musketeers.

"All for one and one for all!" the four friends cried.

Their adventures together had just begun!